I Will Dance

written by
Nancy Bo Flood

illustrated by
Julianna Swaney

 ATHENEUM BOOKS FOR YOUNG READERS
New York London Toronto Sydney New Delhi

Acknowledgments

Thank you to my agent, Rubin Pfeffer, who said, "I know just the right editor for this book," and indeed he did. Thank you, Reka, for being that editor, and Julianna, for creating images that dance right off the pages! My sincere appreciation to Young Dance—the directors, instructors, and especially Eva and all the dancers. You continue to create a community of inclusion and celebration. Truly, you dance in my heart.

—N. B. F.

ATHENEUM BOOKS FOR YOUNG READERS • An imprint of Simon & Schuster Children's Publishing Division • 1230 Avenue of the Americas, New York, New York 10020 • Text copyright © 2020 by Nancy Bo Flood • Illustrations copyright © 2020 by Julianna Swaney • All rights reserved, including the right of reproduction in whole or in part in any form. • ATHENEUM BOOKS FOR YOUNG READERS is a registered trademark of Simon & Schuster, Inc. Atheneum logo is a trademark of Simon & Schuster, Inc. • For information about special discounts for bulk purchases, please contact Simon & Schuster Special Sales at 1-866-506-1949 or business@simonandschuster.com. • The Simon & Schuster Speakers Bureau can bring authors to your live event. • For more information or to book an event, contact the Simon & Schuster Speakers Bureau at 1-866-248-3049 or visit our website at www.simonspeakers.com. • Book design by Karyn Lee • The text for this book was set in Amasis MT. • The illustrations for this book were rendered in watercolor and graphite. • Manufactured in China • 0320 SCP • First Edition • 10 9 8 7 6 5 4 3 2 1 • Library of Congress Cataloging-in-Publication Data • Names: Flood, Nancy Bo, author. | Swaney, Julianna, illustrator. • Title: I will dance / Nancy Bo Flood ; illustrated by Julianna Swaney. • Description: First edition. | New York : Atheneum, [2020] | Summary: Eve's cerebral palsy makes it difficult for her to do many things, but she longs to dance and, finally, her dream is realized. • Includes author's note and information about Young Dance Company. • Identifiers: LCCN 20 19020654| ISBN 9781534430617 (hardcover) | ISBN 9781534430624 (eBook) • Subjects: | CYAC: Dance—Fiction. | Cerebral palsy—Fiction. | People with disabilities—Fiction. • Classification: LCC PZ7.F6618 Iak 2020 | DDC [E]—dc23 LC record available at https://lccn.loc.gov/2019020654

To Megan Flood and Gretchen Pick,
two amazing artists who have enriched
the lives of many through dance

—N. B. F.

To my mom

—J. S.

On my birthday,
can't blow out the candles—
    not enough strength.
But I have one wish:
        a pink tutu.

I want to dance.

I could barely breathe
when I was born.

I was supposed to live
one minute,

maybe two,

not ten years of minutes.

I want to dance, but I can hardly move.

Only my head.

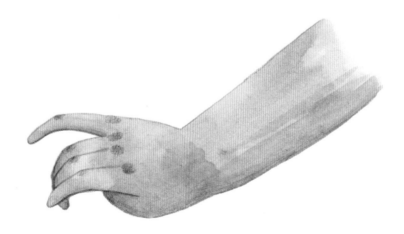

Only my arms and fingers.

I wonder:
How does it feel

to have arms that reach up, up high

legs that walk, skip, run,

like other kids?

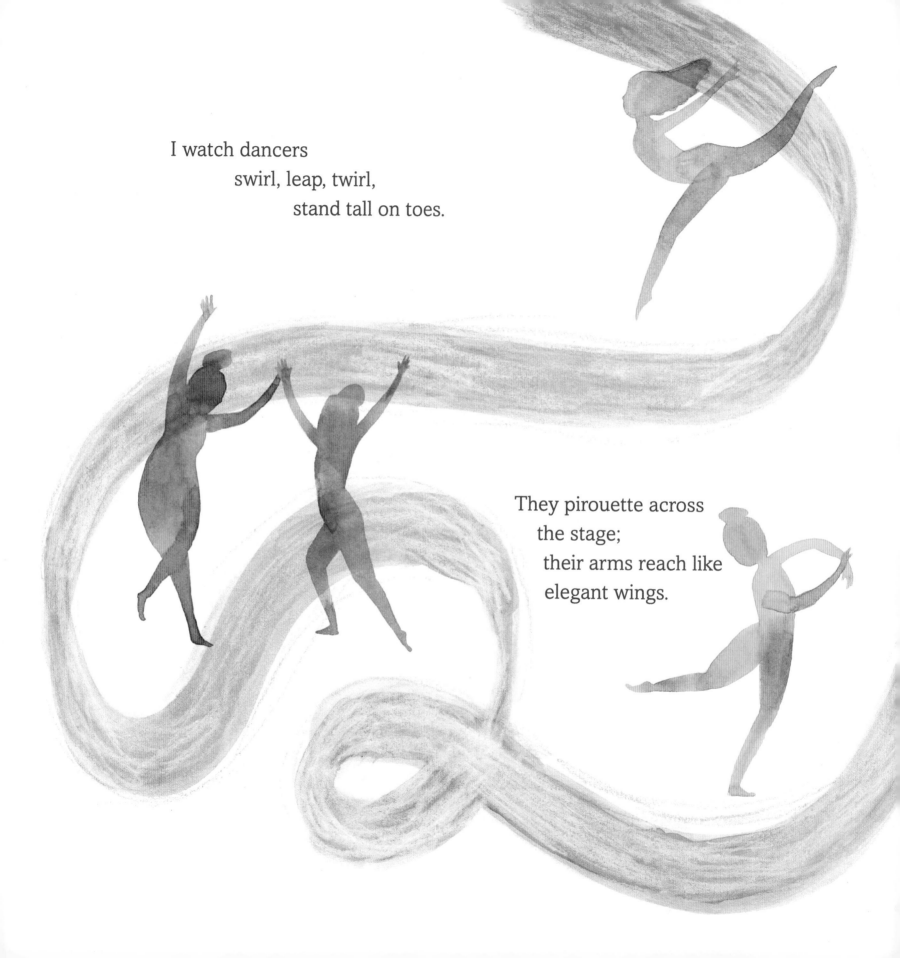

I watch dancers
swirl, leap, twirl,
stand tall on toes.

They pirouette across
the stage;
their arms reach like
elegant wings.

Maybe I could
roll my chair between, around,

while the other dancers
glide past me, tumble over me,
until we are all
mixed together,

one beautiful
laughing heap.

Mom says,
Imagine you are dancing.

I don't want to imagine.
I want to dance.

The teacher says,
Pretend you are dancing.

I don't want to pretend.
I want to move.

I want to feel the music,
sway, swing, fly
over and under.
Together.
Not alone.

I won't give up
my dream of dancing.

How can I dance,
Mom, how?

We will find a way.

Mom reads in the paper:
    Audition for Young Dance—
        all abilities, all ages.
           All are welcome.

All?
I'm not sure.

I'm not ready.
I am safe in my
steel chair,
    stationary wheels,
        a motor,
            me.

What if they stare, whisper,

Not you, not you!

Can't move, can't dance.

Not her!

But I can't help wondering . . .
how would it feel?
I read again, *all abilities, all ages.*

Maybe, maybe . . .

I want to try.

The sign says: *Dance Studio, second floor.*
I roll into the elevator.
Mom pushes the button.

Roll out, down the hall, and then
through an open door.

I see the beautiful wooden floor,
shiny, smooth, like a still pond, waiting,
waiting for dancers, all dancers,

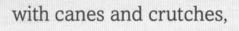

with canes and crutches,

walkers and wheels,

bare feet, slippers, or
callouses—*dancers.*

Not imagine,
not pretend.

Me?

What am I
doing here?

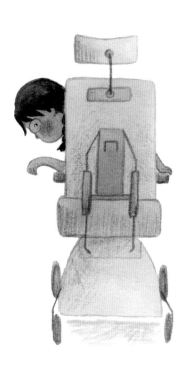

Turn
Around
Run
Away.

Wait.
Dancers pause,
reach toward me.
Welcome!

Welcome?
I roll forward
onto the dance floor.

Join us.
We are many dancers, one circle.
We each pass the touch.

The instructor steps
         toward
              me.

Her eyes meet mine. Her hand opens. She reaches,

dances closer, until her fingers touch mine.

She nods.

Something inside me changes.

I turn
        to the person next to me.

I lift my finger up, then down,
            swirl my fingers around.

He watches, then reaches,
    echoes my movement, adds his own,
        passes the touch, until the circle is complete.

We are all
one circle.

Move to the wall. Make two lines, our instructor says.
Listen to the music, feel the rhythm, count the beats.

One, two, three, my turn, *go!*

Slowly, then faster,
each with a partner, we move across the floor.

We mirror each other, move together, apart,
create space,
create shape,
create dance.

As one,

as *us*,

we dance!

We invent a new move.
Doesn't work, try again.

Try harder, again and again across the smooth floor.
Swoosh, my partner swirls my chair;
I power my wheels, circle with the others.

We move in together, out together.
Again!
We practice, practice, practice.

Performance night!

A belly full of butterflies,
a dressing room full of dancers.

My turn. I roll up to the mirror:
eye shadow, lipstick, then blush.

Now, hurry, hurry, line up!

Hide in the wings.

Lights dim.
A hush falls.

Music begins, swells.
I count the beats.

Breathe!
Heart races, hands sweat,
remember, remember
the movements:
over and under
and around one another,

swirl, glide across the stage, *dance!*
Lights pour over us, pink and gold.
Circles of light, circles of dancers.

Arms link over wheels, connect
into one shape.
Expand.
Contract,
faster, under, over.

I roar, spin my chair,
circle round,
soar.

Lights out.

Stop.

Roll to the front.

Spotlight on.

Listen.

Clapping, whistles, and cheers for me,

for all of us,

together:

Dancers.

Not imagine.
Not pretend.

Not alone.

I dance!

Author's Note

What joy I saw and felt each time I watched a rehearsal or performance of the Young Dance Company. Giggles. Smiles. Laughter. Hugs. I watched dancers of all abilities move across the practice room or across the stage, some in wheelchairs, some with walkers, and some with independent mobility, but each dancer in harmony with the others, each one a part of the whole. At performances, when I looked around at the audience, again what I saw was not pity or sadness, but joy. Tearful joy.

I felt hope as I witnessed the children and adults sharing a passion, sharing friendship, sharing failures and successes.

All of this is what Eva, the real girl who inspired this book, has taught me. Eva was born prematurely, hardly able to breathe or move, and was not expected to live. But like every child, Eva was born with dreams. *Let me try.* With longings. *Let me belong.* And with the desire to be, and to become, herself. Eva. *A dancer.*

About Young Dance,

a note from Gretchen Pick, Executive Director:

Young Dance: Transforming lives through movement

Since 1987, Young Dance has encouraged young people to build body and spirit through the creative art of dance.

Young Dance is an inclusive artistic community of people of all abilities. All dancers are encouraged to push their own individual artistic boundaries. Dancers are invited to be part of a caring, creative community of artists.

Dancers attend class on a weekly basis, and many are also members of the Young Dance Company. This unique performance company of dancers ages seven to eighteen integrates dancers with and without disabilities as equal participants in the exploration, creation, and performance of dance. They engage in artistic inquiries with professional choreographers and with other arts organizations to push the boundaries of the art and practice of dance. For more information, you can visit youngdance.org.